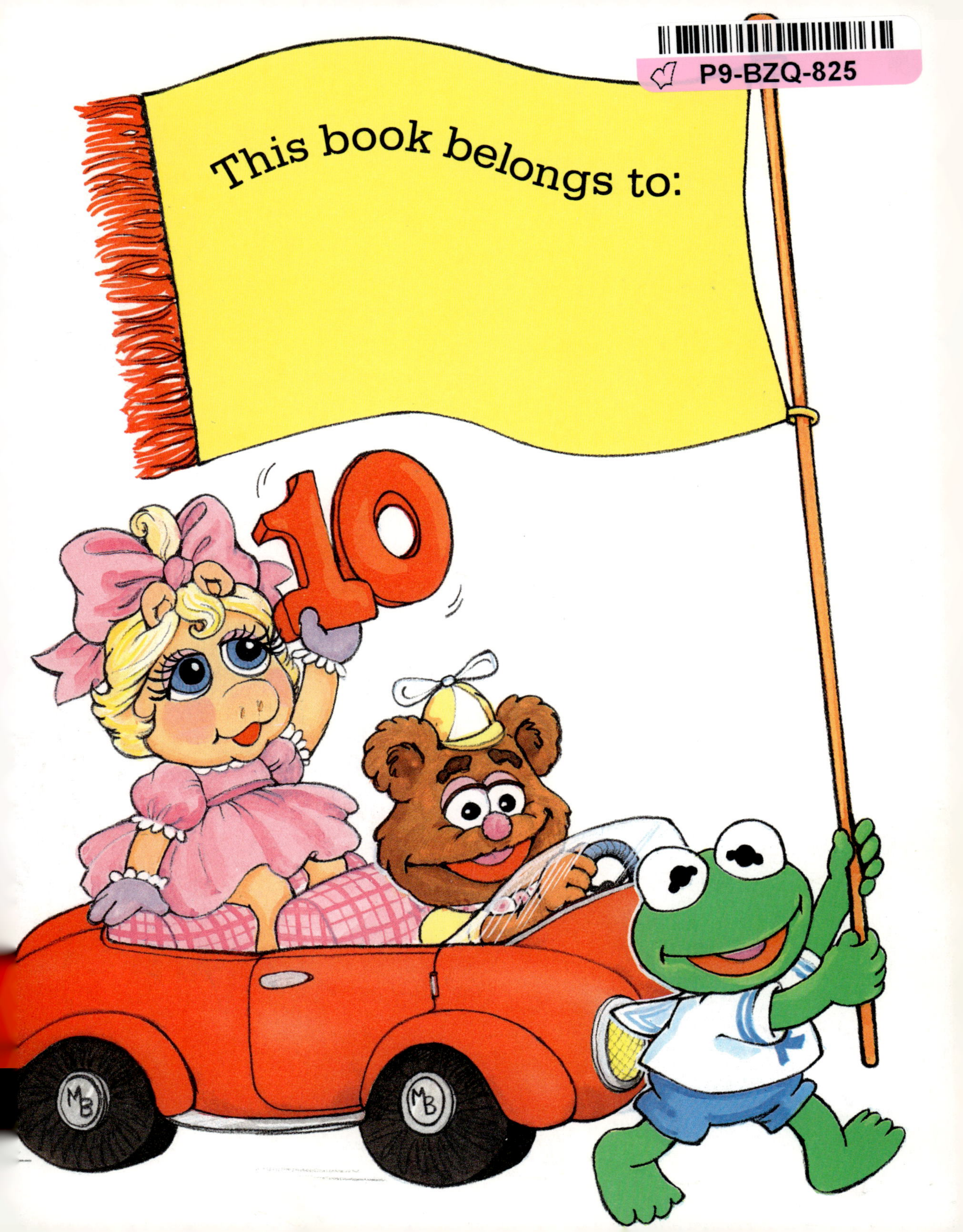
This book belongs to:
10
MB
MB

Published by Grolier Direct Marketing, Danbury, Connecticut

Printed in the U.S.A.

ISBN 0-7172-8276-7

Previously published as 0-681-40838-3

by Bonnie Worth illustrated by Kathy Spahr

crib
trunk
rocking chair
toilet
rocking horse
window
door
armchair
books
sofa
fireplace

sink
picture
mirror
bed
lamp
night table
high chair
curtains
umbrella
clock
teapot

Breakfast
spoon
bib
strawberries
muffin tin
bowl
pitcher
mug
fork
glass
rug
jam
place mat
butt

aucepan
tray
rolls
pot
eggs
plate
napkin
knife
toast
milk
CEREAL
MILK
MILK
salt
cereal
pepper

hat
jacket
dress
Buttons and Bows
scarf
sandals
skirt
boots
raincoat
socks
sweater
bootees

horts
dresser
sneakers
comb
brush
hanger
shirt
slippers
bathrobe
mittens
bow
gloves

tires
gas pump
school bell
school
fire engine
fruit
delivery person
chimney
stroller
menu
table
sundae
Out and About
S GARAGE
Grocery
FIRE ENGI
FLORIS
Fireplace Restaurant
OPEN

dog
police car
cat
traffic light
PET SHOP
POLICE DEPT.
TOY STORE
fire hydrant
toys
TAXI
POST OFFICE
taxi
X207-1
mailbox
plant
window
letter
bus

tomato
straw hat
sun
tractor
On the Farm
crow
corn
chicken
chick
eggs
goat
boots
horse

dle
sheep
bale
of hay
barn
silo
cow
pail
stool
kitten
apple
basket
cat

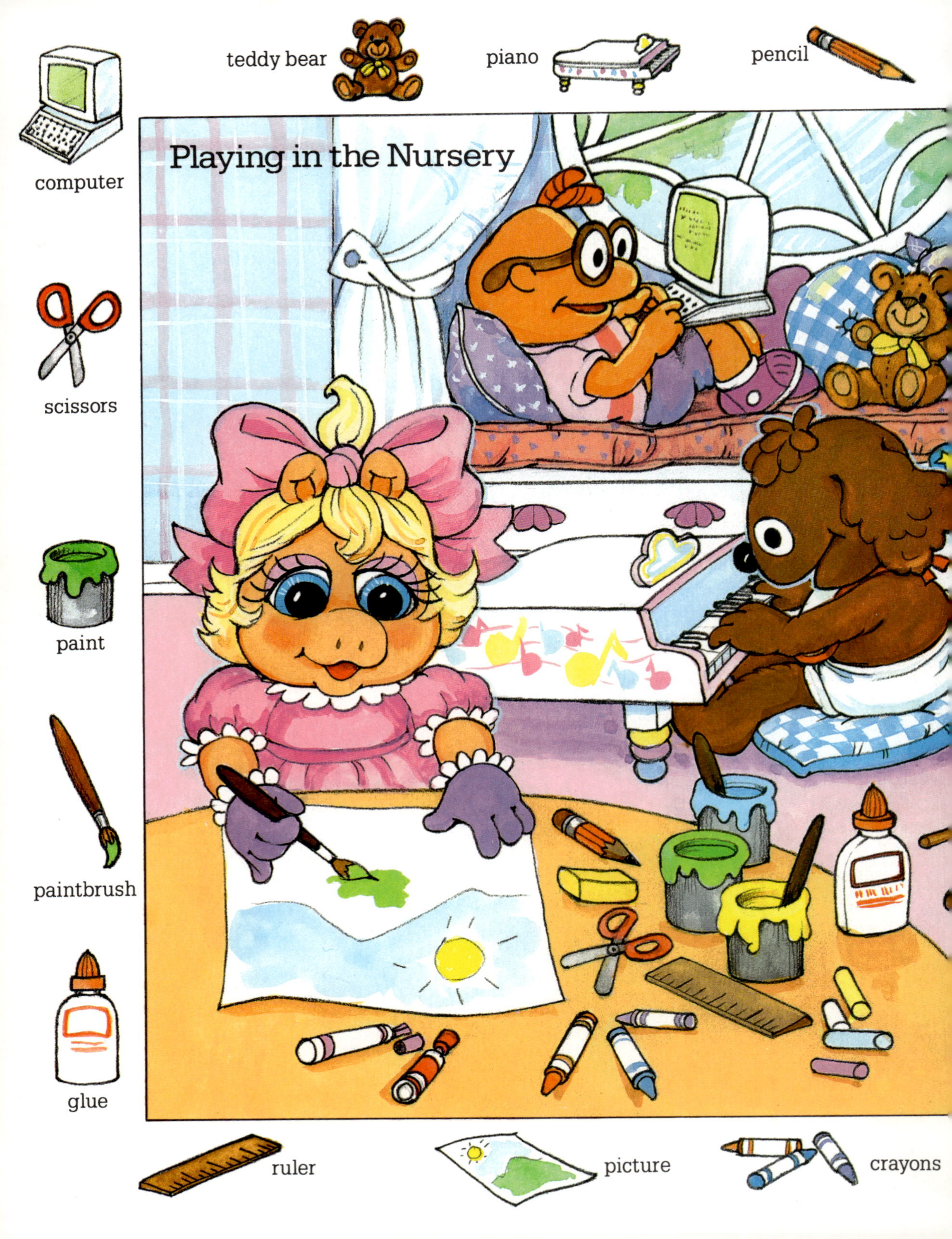
teddy bear
piano
pencil
computer
Playing in the Nursery
scissors
paint
paintbrush
glue
ruler
picture
crayons

chalk
blocks
drum
balloon
bunny
doll
ball
jigsaw
puzzle
tricycle
airplane
yo-yo

rowboat
dog
swan
Strolling Through the Park
sailboat
statue
bird
street lamp
picnic basket
scooter
picnic blanket
pail and shovel

azebo
squirrel
picnic
table
tree
swing
grass
water
fountain
sandbox
bush
bench
flowers

sunglasses
helicopter
bathing suit
At the Beach
lighthouse
SOUVENIRS
beach ball
palm tree
bag
sandals
camera
seashell

y
rubber tube
airplane
fishing rod
beach umbrella
kite
sand castle
fish
starfish
surfboard
lobster

A